Irving, Drumnahaving, Lairg

9SP

D0257436

Irving, Drumnahaving, Lairg

9SP

About This Book

This book is for everyone who is learning their first words in French. By looking at the pictures, it will be easy to read and remember the French words underneath.

When you look at the French words, you will see that in front of most of them, there is **le, la, l'** or **les**, which means "the". When learning French, it is a good idea to learn the **le, la** or **l'** which goes with each one. This is because all words, like table and bed, as well as girl and boy, are feminine or masculine. **La** means the word is feminine and **le** means it is masculine. When **la** or **le** comes in front of a word beginning with **a, e, i, o, u,** or **h**, it usually becomes **l'**. **Les** comes in front of words that are plural; that is more than one, such as tables and beds, and can be either feminine or masculine.

At the back of the book is a guide to help you say all the words in the pictures. But there are some sounds in French which are quite different from any sound in English. To say a French word correctly, you have to hear it spoken first. Listen very carefully and then try to say it that way yourself. But if you say a word as it is written in the guide, a French person will understand you, even if your French accent is not perfect.

First 100 Words In French

Heather Amery
Illustrated by Stephen Cartwright

Translated by Nicole Irving

Cover design by Amanda Barlow

There is a little yellow duck to find in every picture.

Dans la salle de séjour In the living room

Papa
Daddy

Maman
Mummy

le garçon
boy

la fille
girl

le bébé
baby

le chien
dog

le chat
cat

Les vêtements <small>Clothes</small>

le sous-vêtement
<small>vest</small>

la culotte
<small>pants</small>

les chaussures
<small>shoes</small>

les chaussettes
<small>socks</small>

4

le pantalon
trousers

le tee-shirt
t-shirt

le pull-over
jumper

5

Le petit déjeuner Breakfast

le pain
bread

le lait
milk

les oeufs
eggs

la pomme
apple

l'orange
orange

la banane
banana

Dans la cuisine In the kitchen

la table
table

la chaise
chair

l'assiette
plate

le couteau
knife

la fourchette
fork

la cuillère
spoon

la tasse
cup

9

Les jouets Toys

le cheval
horse

le mouton
sheep

la vache
cow

la poule
hen

le cochon
pig

le train
train

les cubes
bricks

Chez Grand-mère et Grand-père At Granny and Grandpa's house

Grand-mère
Granny

Grand-père
Grandpa

les pantoufles
slippers

la robe
dress

le manteau
coat

le chapeau
hat

Au jardin public In the park

l'arbre
tree

la fleur
flower

les balançoires
swings

la balle
ball

14

e toboggan
slide

l'oiseau
bird

les bottes
boots

le bateau
boat

la voiture
car

la bicyclette
bicycle

le camion
truck

l'autobus
bus

l'avion
plane

la maison
house

La fête The party

la glace
ice cream

le gâteau
cake

le ballon
balloon

la pendule
clock

le poisson
fish

les biscuits
biscuits

les bonbons
sweets

A la piscine At the swimming pool

le bras
arm

la main
hand

la jambe
leg

les pieds
feet

les orteils
toes

la tête
head

le derrière
bottom

Au vestiaire
In the changing room

la bouche
mouth

les yeux
eyes

les oreilles
ears

22

le nez
nose

les cheveux
hair

le peigne
comb

la brosse
brush

23

Dans le magasin In the shop

rouge
red

bleu
blue

vert
green

jaune
yellow

rose
pink

blanc
white

noir
black

Dans la salle de bains In the bathroom

le bain
bath

la serviette
towel

les toilettes
toilet

le savon
soap

le ventre
tummy

le canard
duck

Dans la chambre In the bedroom

le lit
bed

la fenêtre
window

la porte
door

la lampe
light

le livre
book

la poupée
doll

l'ours
teddy

Match the words to the pictures

la balle

la banane

les bottes

le canard

le chapeau

le chat

les chaussettes

le chien

le cochon

le couteau

la fenêtre

la fourchette

le gâteau

la glace

le lait

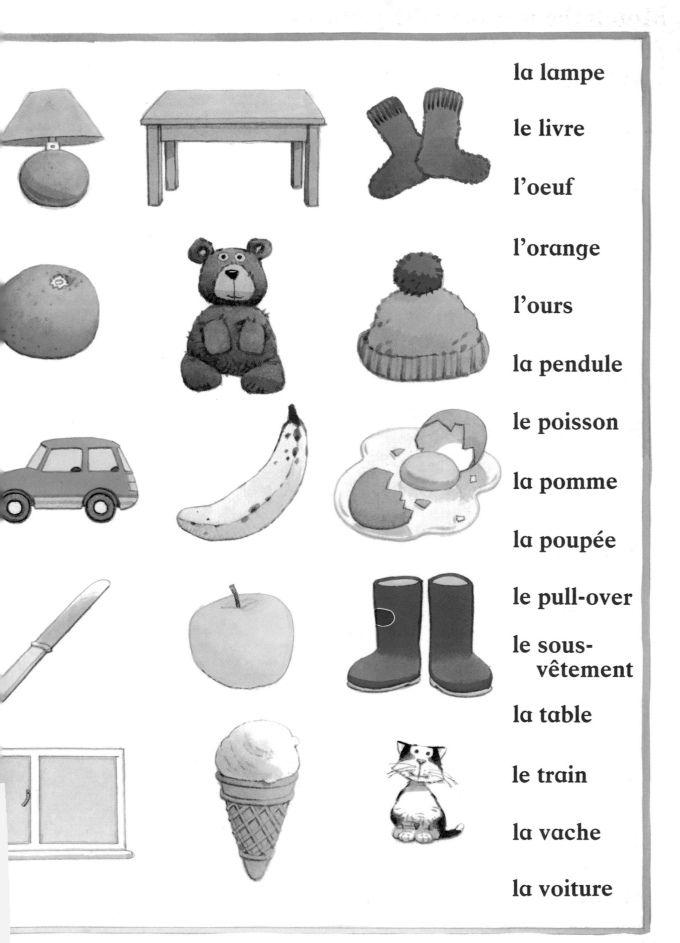

la lampe

le livre

l'oeuf

l'orange

l'ours

la pendule

le poisson

la pomme

la poupée

le pull-over

le sous-
vêtement

la table

le train

la vache

la voiture

Les nombres _{Numbers}

1 **un**
one

2 **deux**
two

3 **trois**
three

4 **quatre**
four

5 **cinq**
five

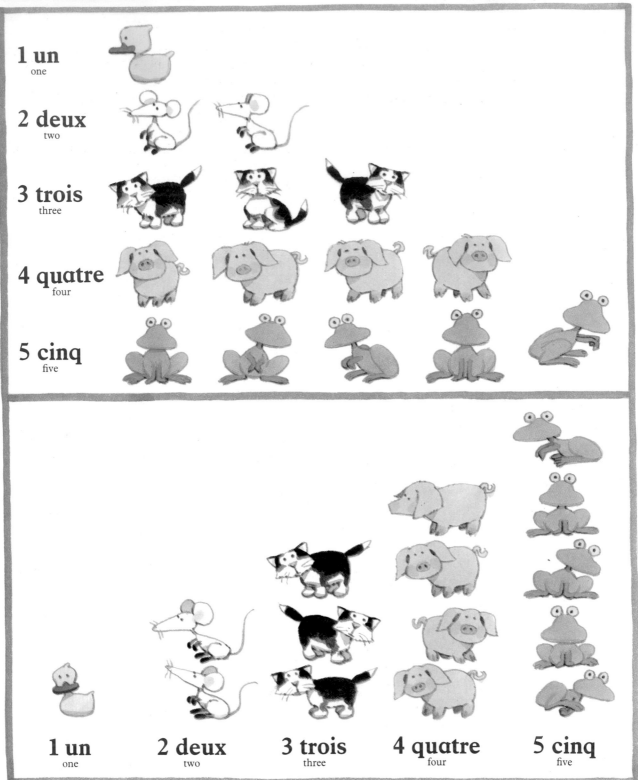

1 **un**
one

2 **deux**
two

3 **trois**
three

4 **quatre**
four

5 **cinq**
five

First published in 1988. © Usborne Publishing Ltd. Printed in Great Britain.

Words in the pictures

In this alphabetical list of all the words in the pictures, the French word comes first, next is the guide to saying the word, and then there is the English translation. The guide may look strange or funny, but just try to read it as if it were English words. It will help you to say the words in French correctly, if you remember these rules:

g is said like *g* in *g*ame
j is said like *s* in trea*s*ure
r is made by growling a little at the back of your throat
n at the end of a word is said right at the back of your nose. There is no sound like it in English
a sounds halfway between the *a* in c*a*t and the *a* in c*a*r
ay is like the *ay* in d*ay*.

l'arbre (m)	*lar-br*	tree
l'assiette (f)	*lass-ee-et*	plate
l'autobus (m)	*lo-toe-bews*	bus
l'avion (m)	*lav-yon*	plane
le bain	*le ban*	bath
les balançoires (f)	*lay bal-an-swar*	swings
la balle	*la bal*	ball
le ballon	*le bu-lon*	balloon
la banane	*la ba-nan*	banana
le bateau	*le bat-toe*	boat
le bébé	*le bay-bay*	baby
la bicyclette	*la bee-see-clet*	bicycle
les biscuits (m)	*lay beese-kwee*	biscuits
blanc	*blon*	white
bleu	*bler*	blue
les bonbons (m)	*lay bon-bon*	sweets
les bottes (f)	*lay bot*	boots
la bouche	*la boosh*	mouth
le bras	*le bra*	arm
la brosse	*la bross*	brush
le camion	*le ca-mee-on*	truck
le canard	*le ca-nar*	duck
la chaise	*la shayz*	chair
la chambre	*la sham-br*	bedroom
le chapeau	*le sha-poe*	hat
le chat	*le sha*	cat
les chaussettes (f)	*lay show-set*	socks
les chaussures (f)	*lay show-sewr*	shoes
le cheval	*le she-val*	horse
les cheveux (m)	*lay sher-ver*	hair
le chien	*le shi-an*	dog
cinq	*sank*	five
le cochon	*le cosh-on*	pig
le couteau	*le coo-toe*	knife

les cubes (m)	*lay kewb*	bricks
la cuillère	*la kwee-yair*	spoon
la cuisine	*la kwee-zeen*	kitchen
la culotte	*la kew-lot*	pants
le derrière	*le dar-ee-air*	bottom
deux	*der*	two
la fenêtre	*la fe-nay-tr*	window
la fête	*la fay-t*	party
la fille	*la fee-ye*	girl
la fleur	*la fler*	flower
la fourchette	*la foor-shet*	fork
le garçon	*le gar-son*	boy
le gâteau	*le ga-toe*	cake
la glace	*la glass*	ice cream
Grand-mère	*gron-mair*	Granny
Grand-père	*gron-pair*	Grandpa
la jambe	*la jamb*	leg
le jardin public	*le jar-dan poo-bleek*	park
jaune	*jawn*	yellow
les jouets (m)	*lay joo-ay*	toys
le lait	*le lay*	milk
la lampe	*la lomp*	light
le lit	*le lee*	bed
le livre	*le lee-vr*	book
le magasin	*le ma-ga-zan*	shop
la main	*la man*	hand
la maison	*la may-zon*	house
Maman	*ma-man*	Mummy
le manteau	*le man-toe*	coat
le mouton	*le moo-ton*	sheep

le nez	*le nay*	nose	la robe	*la rob*	dress
noir	*nwar*	black	rose	*rose*	pink
les nombres (m)	*lay nom-br*	numbers	rouge	*rooj*	red
			la rue	*la roo*	street
l'oeuf (m)	*lerf*	egg			
les oeufs (m)	*lay zer*	eggs	la salle de bains	*la sal-de-ban*	bathroom
l'oiseau (m)	*lwa-zoe*	bird	la salle de séjour	*la sal de say-joor*	sitting room
l'orange (f)	*lor-anj*	orange			
les oreilles (f)	*lay zor-ay*	ears	le savon	*le sa-von*	soap
les orteils (m)	*lay zor-tay*	toes	la serviette	*la sair-vee-et*	towel
l'ours (m)	*loorce*	teddy bear	le sous-vêtement	*le soo-vet-man*	vest
			la table	*la ta-bl*	table
le pain	*le pan*	bread	la tasse	*la tass*	cup
Papa	*pa-pa*	Daddy	le tee-shirt	*le tee-shirt*	tee-shirt
le pantalon	*le pan-ta-lon*	trousers	la tête	*le tet*	head
les pantoufles (f)	*lay pan-too-fl*	slippers	le toboggan	*le tob-og-an*	slide
la pendule	*la pan-dewl*	clock	les toilettes (f)	*lay twal-et*	toilet
le peigne	*le payn-ye*	comb	le train	*le tran*	train
le petit déjeuner	*le pe-tee day-je-nay*	breakfast	trois	*trwa*	three
			un	*an*	one
les pieds (m)	*lay pee-ay*	feet			
la piscine	*la pee-seen*	swimming pool	la vache	*la vash*	cow
			le ventre	*le von-tr*	tummy
le poisson	*le pwa-son*	fish	vert	*vair*	green
la pomme	*la pomm*	apple	le vestiaire	*le vays-tee-air*	changing room
la porte	*la por-t*	door			
la poule	*la pool*	hen	les vêtements (m)	*lay vet-mon*	clothes
la poupée	*la poo-pay*	doll	la voiture	*la vwa-tewr*	car
le pull-over	*le pewl-o-ver*	pullover			
quatre	*ka-tr*	four	les yeux (m)	*layz-yer*	eyes

First published in 1988, Usborne Publishing Ltd, Usborne House, 83–85 Saffron Hill, London EC1N 8RT. © 1991, 1988, Usborne Publishing Ltd.

The name Usborne and the device 🐝 are Trade Marks of Usborne Publishing Ltd. All rights reserved. No part of this publication may be reproduced, stored in a retrieval system or transmitted by any form or by any means, electronic, mechanical photocopy, recording or otherwise, without the prior permission of the publisher. Printed in Great Britain.